Find the donuts on every page!

Also, beware... You may crave
donuts after reading!

To my son, Lincoln, and my husband, Kenny, who have been enjoying "Donuts with Dada" every Saturday since Lincoln could say the word "donut". I love you!

For my brother-in-law, Andrew. Without you, this book would not be here.

Based on a true story... well, mostly.

DONUTS with DaDa

Written & Illustrated by
Emily E. Hughes

Oh, how I long for SATURDAY, The most glorious day of the week! The day that makes me smile so hard, it hurts both of my cheeks!

Yay, SATURDAY! Exciting! Super! Duper!

But it is just...

Monday.
The day I pop a wheelie,
the day I turn into Motor-Man,
the day I zoom over the city.
    It's a fun day,
        but it's no SATURDAY!

"Is tomorrow SATURDAY, Mama?"

"No, silly willy, SATURDAY is still five days away because tomorrow is Tuesday."

Oh, how I long for SATURDAY, The most glorious day of the week! The day that makes me smile so hard, it hurts both of my cheeks!

Yay, SATURDAY! Fantastic! Amazing! Miraculous!

But it is just...

Tuesday.
The day I play with my cousins,
the day I turn into Amaze-Man,
the day I fly across the sky.
It's a fun day, but it's no SATURDAY!

"Is tomorrow SATURDAY, Mama?"

"No, crazy wazy, SATURDAY is still four days away because tomorrow is Wednesday."

Oh, how I long for SATURDAY, The most glorious day of the week! The day that makes me smile so hard, it hurts both of my cheeks!

Yay, SATURDAY! Wonderful! Magnificent! Splendid!

But it is just...

Wednesday.
The day I go to the zoo,
the day I turn into Animal-Man,
the day I swing like the monkeys.
It's a fun day, but it's no SATURDAY!

"Is tomorrow SATURDAY, Mama?"

"No, funky monkey, SATURDAY is still three days away because tomorrow is Thursday."

THURSDAY

Oh, how I long for SATURDAY, The most glorious day of the week! The day that makes me smile so hard, it hurts both of my cheeks!

Yay, SATURDAY! Unbelievable! Joyful! Yipee!

But it is just...

Thursday.
The day I go to the beach,
the day I turn into Captain-Man,
the day I ride a dolphin.
It's a fun day, but it's no SATURDAY!

"Is tomorrow SATURDAY, Mama?"

"No, funny bunny, SATURDAY is still
two days away because
tomorrow is Friday."

Oh, how I long for SATURDAY, The most glorious day of the week! The day that makes me smile so hard, it hurts both of my cheeks!

Yay, SATURDAY! Spectacular! Wild! Catty-wompy!

But it is just...

Friday.
The day I ride my golf cart,
the day I turn into Wonder-Man,
the day I save the world.
It's a fun day, but it's no SATURDAY!

"Is tomorrow SATURDAY, Mama?"

"Actually, YES, poopy loopy, tomorrow IS SATURDAY!"

"WHAAAAAAT??!!"

IT'S SATURDAY!!!
SURPRISING! ASTONISHING! DELICIOUS!!
The most glorious day of the week!
It is...

DONUTS WITH DADA DAY!!!!

Glazed donuts!

Chocolate donuts!

Sprinkle donuts!

Sugar donuts!

Strawberry frosted donuts!

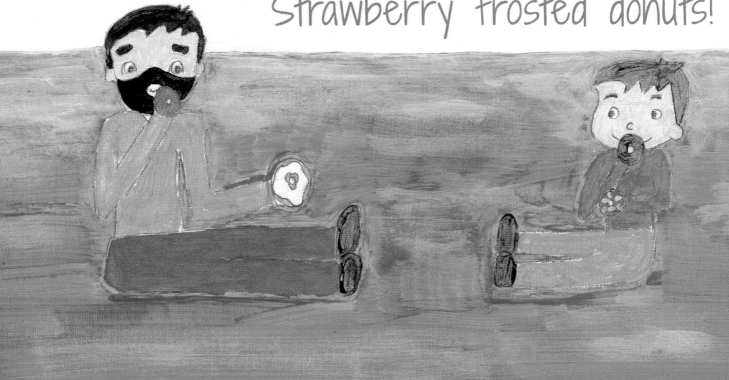

I love donuts, but the best part of SATURDAY is getting to spend the day with DADA!

Well, sometimes Mama is there, too,
that loony toony.

The end.

Made in United States
Orlando, FL
18 September 2024

51663269R00024